HOCKEY SUPERSTARS

AMAZING Forwards

NHL®

P9-API-327

BY

James Duplacey

Kids Can Press

TORONTO

Kids Can Press Ltd. acknowledges with appreciation the assistance of the Canada Council and the Ontario Arts Council in the production of this book.

Canadian Cataloguing in Publication Data

Duplacey, James
      Amazing forwards

(Hockey superstars)
ISBN 1-55074-305-8

1. Hockey players – Biography.
2. National Hockey League – Biography. I. Title. II. Series

GV848.5.A1D85.1996   796.962'092'2   C96-930298-3

Text copyright © 1996 by National Hockey League Enterprises, Inc.;
and Dan Diamond and Associates, Inc.

Kids Can Press Ltd.
29 Birch Avenue
Toronto, Ontario, Canada
M4V 1E2

Edited by Elizabeth MacLeod
Book design and electronic page layout by First Image
Printed and bound in Canada by Printcrafters Inc.

96 0 9 8 7 6 5 4 3 2 1

Photo credits
Harold Barkley: 23 (bottom). **Bruce Bennett Studios:** cover (all), 3 (left, second from left, right), 4 (both), 5 (top and bottom left), 6 (all), 7 (both), 8 (right), 9 (both), 12, 13 (right), 14 (right), 15 (left), 16 (both), 17 (both), 18 (right), 19 (top right), 20 (right), 23 (top), 25 (left), 26 (both), 27 (both), 28 (right), 29 (middle, right), 31 (both), 32 (both), 33 (both), 34 (both), 35 (both), 38 (right), 39 (both), 40 (left, right), back cover (left, middle). **Tony Biegun/The Ice Age:** 21 (bottom right). **Denis Brodeur:** 18 (left), 24 (right), 25 (right), 30. **Michael Burns:** 37 (bottom left). **Dan Hamilton:** 5 (top right), 13 (left), back cover (right). **Hockey Hall of Fame:** 15 (right), 20 (left), 21 (top right). **Imperial Oil Turofsky Collection/Hockey Hall of Fame:** 3 (second from right), 10 (left), 19 (bottom right), 29 (left), 36 (both), 37 (top left). **Doug MacLellan/Hockey Hall of Fame:** 5 (bottom right), 8 (left), 28 (left), 38 (left), 40 (middle). **NHL Publishing:** 21 (left), 24 (left). **Frank Prazak/Hockey Hall of Fame:** 10 (right), 11 (both), 14 (left), 19 (left), 22, 37 (right).

CONTENTS

INTRODUCTION		4
YOUNG GUNS:	Lindros, Jagr	6
THE EUROPEANS:	Fedorov, Zhamnov, Bure, Forsberg	8
STRENGTH DOWN CENTRE:	Béliveau, Esposito	10
THE MAGNIFICENT:	Lemieux	12
SMALL SIZE, HUGE HEARTS:	Henri Richard, Fleury, Joliat	14
PLAYMAKERS:	Ratelle, Perreault, Francis, Oates,	16
THE SHOOTERS:	Bossy, Mahovlich	18
FAMOUS FIRSTS:	Malone, Mullen, Sittler, Clapper, Selanne	20
MR. HOCKEY:	Howe	22
THE COURAGEOUS:	Gilbert, Clarke	24
DRIVE AND DETERMINATION:	McDonald, Bucyk, Dionne, Gartner	26
THE GOLDEN JET AND BRETT:	Brett Hull, Bobby Hull	28
THE 2000-POINT SCORER:	Gretzky	30
LEGENDS:	Mikita, Lafleur	32
TEAM PLAYERS:	Goulet, Yzerman, Savard, Hawerchuk	34
THE ROCKET:	Maurice Richard	36
CENTRES OF ATTENTION:	Gilmour, Messier, Trottier	38
FUTURE FABS:	Bondra, Tkachuk, LeClair	40

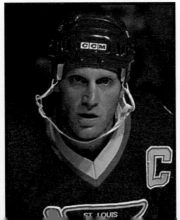

RRRRoaarr

The centreman speeds across the blue line, then slams on the brakes, spraying a shower of ice chips into the air. Tonight he doesn't hear the roar of the crowd. Tonight he hears only his left-winger calling for the puck. He passes it off, then makes a break for the net. His teammate steers the puck around the defence and shoots back a soft pass right onto the centreman's stick. With a snap of the wrists, the centre sends the puck soaring towards the net. The goaltender throws out a glove hand but catches only air as the puck flies past him.

For a moment there is silence, but when the fans see the red light go on, they erupt with an explosive roar. The centreman's teammates pour off the bench, slapping his back and grabbing his arm. The centreman has just scored the game-winning goal, giving his team a hard-earned victory and a much-needed win. This goal won a game for his team and sent the fans home happy. And every amazing forward will tell you there's no better feeling than that.

One of the happiest moment of Lanny McDonald's life was when his team won the Stanley Cup. "I could have carried that Cup forever," said this amazing forward.

No doubt about it, Wayne Gretzky has definitely earned the title the "Great One." He has won 36 individual NHL awards and continues to play hard.

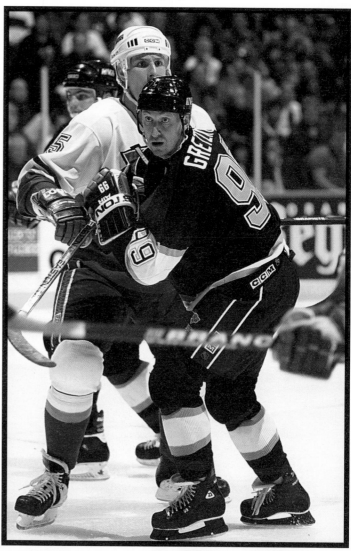

Although Sergei Fedorov only joined the NHL in 1990, he has already won the Selke Trophy, Pearson Award and Hart Trophy, as well as playing in several All-Star games.

Mario Lemieux's teammates are quick to congratulate him whenever he scores a goal. Did you know that "Mario the Magnificent" scored a goal on his very first NHL shift?

Eric Lindros has the size, speed, strength and smarts of a superstar. In 1995 he won the Hart Trophy as the NHL's most valuable player.

An amazing forward during the regular season and the playoffs, Bobby Clarke led the Philadelphia Flyers to two Stanley Cup wins.

YOUNG GUNS

Eric Lindros

Centre — Philadelphia

To become a young gun in the NHL, a player must have speed, size and strength. In the 1994–95 season, Eric Lindros showed he had all three. He helped the Philadelphia Flyers reach the NHL Conference Finals for the first time in six years and he also led the team in six scoring categories.

Even though he won the Hart Trophy as the NHL's most valuable player in 1994–95, Lindros was not satisfied. "The most important thing is to win the Stanley Cup," he says. "That's it, that's where it's at." Lindros is prepared to sacrifice individual achievement for team success, and that's what makes him one of the NHL's top stars.

"He has just scratched the surface in terms of his dominance."
Craig MacTavish, 1995
Teammate

Lindros has a passion for hockey that sets him apart. He has overcome several knee injuries to become the game's top young star.

Jaromir Jagr

Right Wing — Pittsburgh

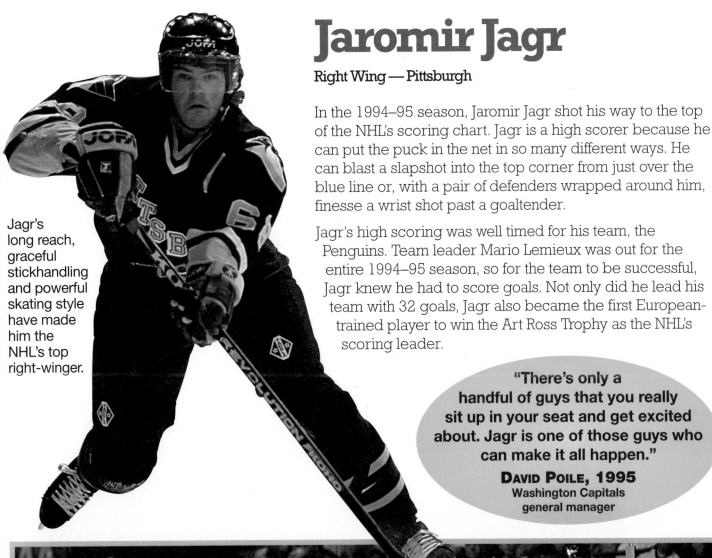

Jagr's long reach, graceful stickhandling and powerful skating style have made him the NHL's top right-winger.

In the 1994–95 season, Jaromir Jagr shot his way to the top of the NHL's scoring chart. Jagr is a high scorer because he can put the puck in the net in so many different ways. He can blast a slapshot into the top corner from just over the blue line or, with a pair of defenders wrapped around him, finesse a wrist shot past a goaltender.

Jagr's high scoring was well timed for his team, the Penguins. Team leader Mario Lemieux was out for the entire 1994–95 season, so for the team to be successful, Jagr knew he had to score goals. Not only did he lead his team with 32 goals, Jagr also became the first European-trained player to win the Art Ross Trophy as the NHL's scoring leader.

> "There's only a handful of guys that you really sit up in your seat and get excited about. Jagr is one of those guys who can make it all happen."
>
> **DAVID POILE, 1995**
> Washington Capitals
> general manager

THE EUROPEANS

Sergei Fedorov

Centre — Detroit

Sergei Fedorov's European training taught him to be a tireless worker at both ends of the ice. Fedorov combines offensive flair with determined defensive play. In 1993–94, he became the first player to win the Hart Trophy as league MVP and the Selke Trophy as the league's best defensive forward in the same season.

Alexei Zhamnov

Centre — Winnipeg

Like many of the European players who are NHL stars, Alexei Zhamnov has a flair for both goal-scoring and passing. He can slip a pass to a teammate through a maze of skates and sticks, or use his speed to deke a defender for a shot on goal. In 1994–95, Zhamnov led the Jets in scoring and earned a berth on the NHL's Second All-Star Team.

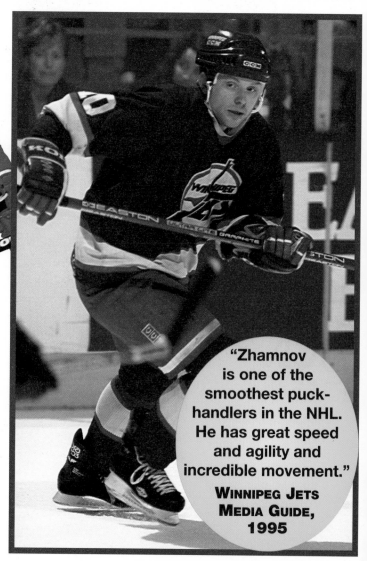

"It's my responsibility to play the best that I can and to concentrate on my defensive work."
SERGEI FEDOROV, 1994

"Zhamnov is one of the smoothest puck-handlers in the NHL. He has great speed and agility and incredible movement."
WINNIPEG JETS MEDIA GUIDE, 1995

Pavel Bure

Right Wing — Vancouver

European players have always been known for their speed. Perhaps the fastest player today is Pavel Bure, the "Russian Rocket." Bure can outrace defenders to reach a puck or sweep by a close-checking forward to create a scoring chance. Dedicated training has helped Bure develop the effortless skating style that has become his trademark.

Peter Forsberg

Centre — Quebec, Colorado

Peter Forsberg is part of the new breed of European players. He isn't afraid to go into the corners to dig out the puck or deliver a bone-crunching bodycheck. Forsberg stayed in Sweden until he was 22, maturing and developing his skills. When he finally arrived in the NHL, Forsberg won the Calder Trophy as the NHL's top rookie.

"Sometimes the things he does on the ice leave the whole bench in awe."
GINO ODJICK, 1995
Teammate

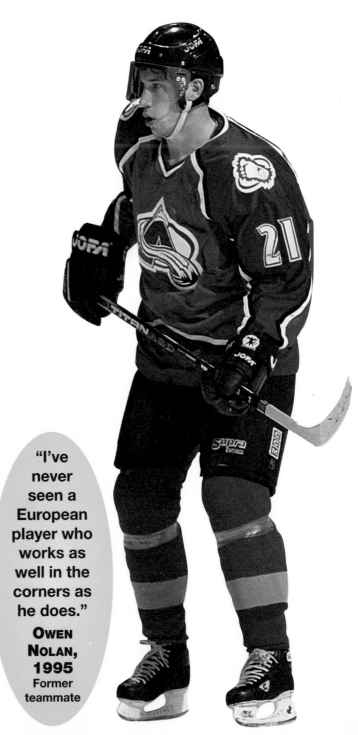

"I've never seen a European player who works as well in the corners as he does."
OWEN NOLAN, 1995
Former teammate

STRENGTH DOWN CENTRE

Jean Béliveau

Centre — Montreal

When he joined the Montreal Canadiens in 1953–54, Jean Béliveau was the biggest centreman—190 cm (6 ft. 3 in.) and 93 kg (205 lb.)—in the NHL. With his long reach, he could easily deke opposing goaltenders. And with his size, he could also outmuscle defenders for rebounds or loose pucks.

For 20 seasons, Béliveau wore the Canadiens uniform and was captain for ten of those years. He played on ten Stanley Cup-winning teams and was selected as the NHL's All-Star centreman ten times. Béliveau was the second NHL player to score 1000 points and the first to be awarded playoff MVP honours.

Béliveau's famed number 4 was retired by the Montreal Canadiens in 1973.

> "Everyone demands more of himself in our uniform. Everyone is brought in knowing he must sacrifice himself for the good of the team. Individual honours are unimportant next to team honours."
>
> JEAN BÉLIVEAU, 1969

Béliveau was a Canadien throughout his entire career. In 1972 he was elected to the Hockey Hall of Fame

Phil Esposito

Centre — Chicago, Boston, NY Rangers

From 1969 to 1975, Phil Esposito was the "big guy" for Boston in more ways than one. At 188 cm (6 ft. 2 in.) and 94 kg (208 lb.), he was the biggest player on the team and he scored the "biggest" goals. "Espo" wasn't a great skater, but he was a top scorer because once he got in the slot he was hard to move out. He led the Bruins in power-play and game-winning goals three times and led all playoff goal scorers in 1970 and 1972, when the Bruins won the Stanley Cup.

In 1970–71 Espo had 550 shots on goal, a record no player has come close to matching. And he's still a big man in hockey. In 1991 Espo became president and general manager of the Tampa Bay Lightning.

> "I always used to tell myself when I went out on the ice, 'I gotta believe, I gotta believe I'm the best out there.'"
> **PHIL ESPOSITO, 1986**

The Magnificent

Mario Lemieux

Centre — Pittsburgh

"Mario the Magnificent" is an all-around superstar: a champion, a leader, and a hero to millions of hockey fans. Lemieux is known as the Magnificent because no one can score more goals in as many different ways as he can. He showed that versatility in a 1991 game when he became the first player to score five goals in one game in five different ways: on the power play, at even strength, on a breakaway, on a penalty shot, and into the empty net.

Although Lemieux has had to overcome injuries in five of his ten NHL seasons, he has still emerged as a dominant player. He has won five scoring titles and in 1992 became only the second player in NHL history to be named the MVP in the playoffs two years in a row.

In 1993 Lemieux had another barrier to climb when he was diagnosed as having Hodgkin's disease, a form of cancer. Instead of feeling sorry for himself, he immediately underwent treatment for the disease and began planning for his return to action. Just six weeks later, Lemieux returned to the Penguins lineup and averaged more than three points a game. He missed the 1994–95 season with a back injury but returned to action with the Penguins in 1995–96.

Lemieux has proven himself to be not only a magnificent athlete but one of the most courageous ever.

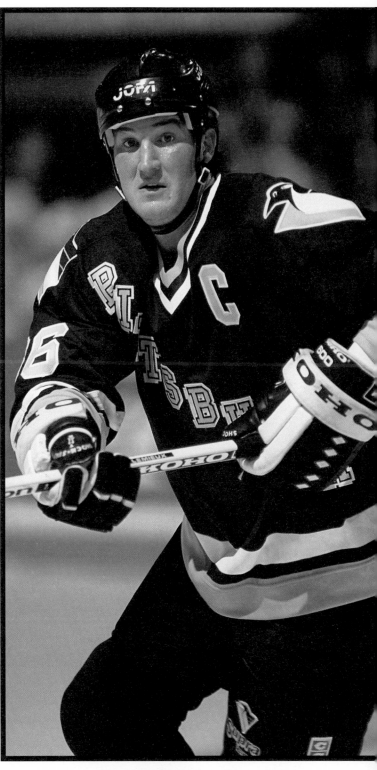

"I'm not coming back to be an average player. I want to be one of the top players in the world. I think I can get my game back to where it was a couple of years ago."
MARIO LEMIEUX, 1995

SMALL SIZE, HUGE HEARTS

Henri Richard

Centre — Montreal

Henri Richard stands only 170 cm (5 ft. 7 in.) and weighed 73 kg (160 lb.) when he played, but he still had 20 high-scoring years in the NHL. His great skating and stickhandling made him one of the best forecheckers and penalty killers. Of course, playing on the same line as his top-scoring brother, Maurice "Rocket" Richard, for part of his career helped too.

In the four seasons the "Pocket Rocket" was the Canadiens captain, the team won the Stanley Cup once and finished first twice. Richard played on 11 Stanley Cup winners, more times than any other player has been on the winning team.

"Henri belongs right up there with Howe, Hull, the 'Rocket,' Béliveau and all the rest. He is a true superstar."
SAM POLLOCK, 1973
Former Montreal Canadiens general manager

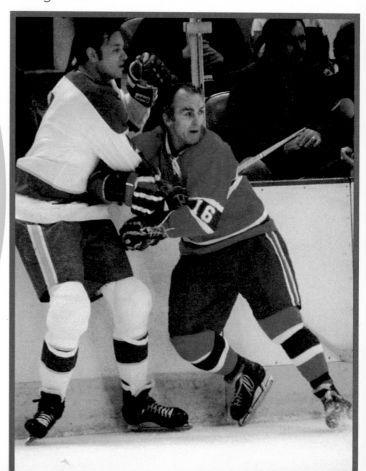

Theoren Fleury

Right Wing — Calgary

No one gave Theoren Fleury much of a chance to make it to the NHL. After all, he stands only 168 cm (5 ft. 6 in.) tall. But, thanks to his determination, he has become one of the league's biggest stars.

Fleury makes his size work for him. His low centre of balance makes it hard for defenders to knock him off the puck. As well, his speed allows him to reach loose pucks and rebounds. Fleury's courage and determination have made him an inspiration to every young player hoping to make it to the "big" league.

"I admire his competitiveness, his strength and his high skill level. And his heart more than makes up for his size."
MIKE KEENAN, 1995
St. Louis Blues
general manager

Aurel Joliat

Left Wing — Montreal

Although he weighed only 61 kg (136 lb.) and stood 168 cm (5 ft. 6 in.), Aurel Joliat played 16 years with the Montreal Canadiens. He lasted that long because of his incredible stamina. Joliat sometimes played an entire game without coming off the ice. No wonder they called him the "Mighty Atom."

Joliat worked hard to become the league's sharpest skater, surest shooter and prettiest passer. That determination on the ice carried him all the way to the Hockey Hall of Fame.

"Joliat was a wizard with the stick. He could skate, turn and score from any position. And, despite his size, he had the heart of a lion."
FRANK SELKE SR., 1955
Montreal Canadiens
general manager

PLAYMAKERS

Jean Ratelle

Centre — NY Rangers, Boston

Jean Ratelle played 1281 games in the NHL and impressed everyone with his dedication and style. He was a great playmaker, collecting more assists than goals in 17 of his 21 NHL seasons. From 1968 to 1980, Ratelle scored at least 25 goals and averaged 50 assists each season.

"Style, class, élan, grace, dignity and elegance. Don't forget gentleman. Add skill, intelligence, instinct, ambition. That is Jean Ratelle."

FRANK ORR, 1980
Sportswriter

Gilbert Perreault

Centre — Buffalo

Gilbert Perreault collected more assists than goals in 15 of his 17 NHL seasons. He was a smooth-skating playmaker who had a real talent for finding a teammate who was open to take a pass. Perreault spent his entire career with the Buffalo Sabres, and his famed number 11 was the first the Sabres have ever retired.

"He's the biggest leader on this team. He always gives 100 per cent and he can do everything so well."

JERRY KORAB, 1986
Teammate

Ron Francis

Centre — Hartford, Pittsburgh

It's all in the hands for super centre Ron Francis. His quick reflexes have made him one of the NHL's top face-off men. By winning the draw, Francis can set up his teammates for a shot on goal or clear the puck from his own zone. He has never set up fewer than 43 goals in a single season and has averaged more than 55 assists a year.

> "I'm not the fastest skater in the league, so I have to use anticipation and rely on my instincts. If you're not willing to work hard at it, there's no way you can do it."
> **RON FRANCIS, 1994**

Adam Oates

Centre — Detroit, St. Louis, Boston

The secret to Adam Oates's success as a playmaker lies in his stickhandling ability. The puck seems to be glued to the blade of his stick, allowing Oates to feather a backhand pass or drill a forward feed anywhere on the ice. In 1992–93, he set up 97 goals to become only the third forward to record more than 95 assists in a single season.

> "His passing ability is the best in the league. He waits and waits until he sees a guy in perfect position. I've never seen anyone make a backhand pass like he can."
> **STEVE YZERMAN, 1993**
> **Former teammate**

THE SHOOTERS

Mike Bossy

Right Wing — NY Islanders

Mike Bossy not only had the most accurate shot of any NHL player but he had the quickest wrist shot as well. He used that rapid-fire release to become the first rookie to score 50 goals in one season.

But there was more to Bossy than just his shot. He also had an unteachable sense that allowed him to get into the open for a shot on goal. That sense helped Bossy lead the Islanders in shots in eight of his ten seasons with the team.

Bossy scored at least 50 goals in each of his first nine NHL seasons, a feat no player has equalled. He was the second player to score 50 goals in 50 games and was also a fine playmaker, collecting a total of 553 assists.

Bossy was a three-time Lady Byng Trophy winner and became a member of the Hockey Hall of Fame in 1991.

"He's got amazing quickness. Usually, if a goaltender has a split second to set himself, he's got a chance. But not on a shot like Bossy's got."
TONY ESPOSITO, 1978
Goalie

Frank Mahovlich

Left Wing — Toronto, Detroit, Montreal

In 1981 Frank Mahovlich earned his greatest honour when he became a member of the Hockey Hall of Fame.

Frank Mahovlich captured the hearts of hockey fans in Toronto, Detroit and Montreal with his graceful skating and powerful shot. All eyes would be on the "Big M" as he crossed the blue line and wound up to take one of his booming shots. He would slowly draw his stick back high above his head before following through with a sizzling slapshot. That style helped the Leafs win four Stanley Cups and made the Big M one of the game's most popular players.

When Mahovlich was traded to Detroit in 1968, horrified Leaf fans paraded around Maple Leaf Gardens to mourn their loss. Three seasons later, the Big M was traded to Montreal, where he won two more Stanley Cups and played some of his best hockey.

"No one puts more into a game than Frank. He makes it all look so easy. But watch the guys trying to catch him. That will show you how fast he's skating."
PETER MAHOVLICH, 1973
Brother and teammate

FAMOUS FIRSTS

Joe Malone

The First Scoring Leader

Joe Malone was a smooth-skating centre who had so many great moves on the ice that he was known as the "Phantom." He became the NHL's first scoring champion, notching 44 goals in only 20 games in 1917–18. Malone's average of 2.2 goals per game in one season is still an NHL record.

Joe Mullen

The First 1000-Point American

Although he didn't learn to skate until he was a teenager, Joe Mullen always dreamed of playing in the NHL. He spent three years in the minors, but his hard work and dedication finally paid off. On February 7, 1995, this native of New York City became the first player born in the U.S. to score 1000 points in the NHL.

Darryl Sittler
The First Ten-Point Game

On February 7, 1976, Darryl Sittler set an NHL record that no player has been able to beat. Sittler's luck (he scored one goal from behind the net) and skill (three goals on three shots) allowed him to collect six goals and four assists as the Toronto Maple Leafs downed the Boston Bruins 11–4.

Dit Clapper
The First 20-Year Man

It takes skill, stamina and a bit of luck to play 20 years in the NHL. Dit Clapper had all three. He began his career with Boston in 1927 and didn't retire until 1946. Clapper is also the only player to be an All-Star as both a forward and a defenceman. He was an All-Star right-winger twice and an All-Star defenceman four times.

Teemu Selanne
The First 70-Goal Rookie

No rookie in NHL history has had the impact of Teemu Selanne. Thanks to his natural instincts, sharp reflexes and quick acceleration, the "Finnish Flash" set rookie records for goals (76) and points (132). In 1992–93 Selanne became only the ninth NHL player to score 70 goals in a single season.

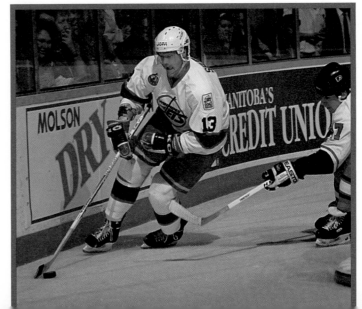

Mr. Hockey

"I'm retiring,
but not quitting.
I hate the word quit."
GORDIE HOWE,
1980

Gordie Howe

Right Wing — Detroit, Hartford

He was called "Mr. Hockey." Gordie Howe played in the NHL for 26 seasons, setting records for goals, assists and points, as well as for seasons and games played, to name just a few. He also finished among the top five scorers in the NHL for 18 straight seasons. What's so amazing about that? Only 32 players in NHL history have even played for 18 seasons!

Howe started his career in 1946 with the Detroit Red Wings. Then, in the 1950 playoffs, he suffered a serious head injury and underwent numerous operations to save his life. But when he returned to action the next season, Howe was more determined to succeed. He won a total of six MVP awards and six scoring titles and led the Red Wings to four Stanley Cups. During the 1960s, Howe served as the Red Wings' captain, and was also the team's assistant coach. And he kept playing. And playing.

In 1971 Howe retired, but he returned in 1973 to play with his sons, Mark and Marty, with the Houston Aeros in the World Hockey Association. Later he came back to the NHL to play with his sons in Hartford.

Mr. Hockey played 32 seasons of professional hockey, a record that will probably never be broken. In his last season, at the age of 52, Howe played in all 80 games. He may have retired, but he never quit.

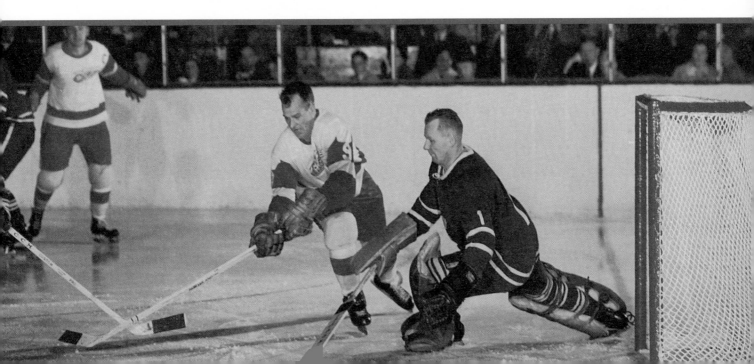

THE
COURAGEOUS

"If there was one thrill during my career, it was coming back from both of those back operations. One spinal fusion is bad enough. But to have two and bounce back to play, I think I'm a lucky guy."
ROD GILBERT,
1984

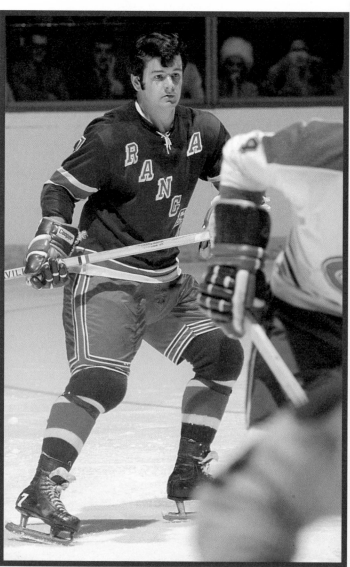

Rod Gilbert

Right Wing — NY Rangers

Can you believe that Rod Gilbert broke his back and still played 18 years in the NHL? It takes a man with incredible courage to overcome such an injury.

Gilbert underwent two long operations to heal his back. He almost lost a leg when complications arose during one of those operations. Then he not only had to learn to skate again, he had to learn to walk too. But Gilbert persevered to become one of the Rangers' top players ever.

When he retired in 1977, Gilbert had set or tied 20 team records for the Rangers. He won the Masterton Trophy in 1976 for "best exemplifying the qualities of perseverance, sportsmanship and dedication to hockey."

Bobby Clarke

Centre — Philadelphia

The fact that Bobby Clarke even played hockey shows his courage. When he was a teenager, Clarke discovered he had diabetes. Although he was told he would probably never play professionally, Clarke never gave up on his dream to make the NHL.

Clarke joined Philadelphia in 1969 and quickly proved that he was a star. His courage inspired his teammates, who gave an extra effort when they saw how hard Clarke was working.

After he retired, Clarke served as general manager of the Flyers and the Minnesota North Stars. In 1992 he was named the first general manager of the Florida Panthers. Clarke returned to the Flyers as club president and general manager in 1994.

"[Clarke] embodies so many things. What will be recognized is his attitude, his dedication, his courage. We'll remember him because he is a superlative individual."

PAT QUINN, 1981
Former Philadelphia Flyers coach

DRIVE AND DETERMINATION

Lanny McDonald

Right Wing — Toronto, Colorado, Calgary

Lanny McDonald was determined to achieve three things in his career: 500 goals, 1000 points and the Stanley Cup. He accomplished all his aims, not only leading the Flames to the Stanley Cup in 1989 but also scoring a key goal in the last game of the finals. McDonald believed that nothing could be achieved without sacrifice and effort. That work ethic was an inspiration to all his teammates.

"You need a drive and desire to stay in the game and stay at a competitive level."
LANNY McDONALD, 1989

Johnny Bucyk

Left Wing — Detroit, Boston

When the Bruins won the Stanley Cup in 1970 and 1972, Bobby Orr and Phil Esposito got most of the attention. But they would agree that the credit for those Cup wins should have been shared with the team's oldest player, Johnny Bucyk. Bucyk was called the "Chief" because younger players looked to him for leadership. In 1971, at age 35, he became the oldest player to have a 100-point season.

"I've never considered myself as a glamour guy. I've just gone along, giving my all and getting what I could out of every game."
JOHNNY BUCYK, 1978

Marcel Dionne

Centre — Detroit, Los Angeles, NY Rangers

An NHL great for 18 seasons, Marcel Dionne is the third-highest scorer ever. He was a leading scorer because he had such a quick release on his shot. Dionne was also a powerful skater who was difficult to knock down. He had a total of eight 100-point seasons and at least 50 assists in 14 seasons.

"Marcel Dionne is a superstar, an out-and-out superstar. Some of the things he can do on the ice are unbelievable."
PHIL ESPOSITO, 1987
New York Rangers general manager

Mike Gartner

Right Wing — Washington, Minnesota, NY Rangers, Toronto

Mike Gartner is one of the NHL's most consistent performers. In 1991–92, he became the first player to record his 500th goal, 500th assist, 1000th point and 1000th game all in the same season.

Gartner started his career with Washington and still holds the Capitals' record for career goals, assists and points. During the 1995–96 season, the great Gartner became the first player to score at least 30 goals in 16 seasons.

"He's always been a gritty player who plays hard at both ends of the rink. He's had a wonderful career."
KEVIN LOWE, 1993
Former teammate

THE GOLDEN JET AND BRETT

Brett Hull

Right Wing — Calgary, St. Louis

He shares his father's good looks, bullet shot and impressive scoring skills. Yet Brett Hull plays a very different game than his father did. Bobby Hull played a power game but Brett plays a patient game. He lets his defencemen set up the play while he slides in and out of the action. Before you know it, he's in the open with the puck on his stick. Then, with a snap of his wrists, the puck is on its way into the net.

Brett has one of the quickest releases and most accurate shots in the NHL. That skill has helped him score more goals over the past six seasons than any other player.

"He's like a shark out there. He can smell a hat trick."
MIKE RICHTER, 1993
New York Rangers goaltender

Brett and Bobby Hull are the only father and son to have both been awarded the Hart Trophy as the NHL's most valuable player.

Bobby Hull

Left Wing — Chicago, Winnipeg, Hartford

Bobby Hull was known as the "Golden Jet" because of his hair (blond), skating (fast) and slapshot (even faster). Hull was the first player to score more than 50 goals in a season, firing 54 goals in 1965–66. He was named to the All-Star team in 12 of his 16 NHL seasons and led the league in goals seven times. And no wonder. Hull was an incredibly powerful skater and shooter. His slapshot was clocked at 200 km/h (120 miles per hour), or about 20 per cent faster than anyone else's!

The Golden Jet truly loved his fans. He spent hours signing autographs and appearing at charity events, and he still does. This amazing forward won the Hart Trophy as the NHL's most valuable player twice, the Lady Byng (for most sportsmanlike conduct) once and the Art Ross (for top scorer) three times.

"He is the rare superstar who treats everyone alike: the coaches, the players, the fans and the writers. He'll stand for an hour after a game signing autographs. And he'll smile while he's doing it."

BILLY REAY, 1968
Former Chicago Black Hawks coach

THE 2000-POINT SCORER

"No player in the history of the game has had such an edge over his contemporaries."

SCOTTY BOWMAN, 1987

Detroit Red Wings Director of Personnel/Coach

Wayne Gretzky

Centre — Edmonton, Los Angeles, St. Louis

There is one thing no one will never be able to take away from Wayne Gretzky: he is, and will always be, the "Great One." No one in any sport has set more records than he has — he holds or shares 61 NHL records.

It took Gretzky only 424 games to reach the 1000-point mark, the fastest anyone has ever reached that milestone. He led the NHL in assists for 13 straight seasons, and his assist total alone would rank him among the NHL's all-time scoring leaders.

What makes Gretzky so great? He's not big or fast, his shot is ordinary, and his style isn't smooth. But "No. 99" has an incredible talent for playing hockey. He has even said that he sees plays happening in slow motion, so it's easy for him to anticipate where the puck is headed. The hard work Gretzky has put into practising also helps — a lot.

The Great One thinks there's another reason for his scoring success. When he was six, his dad hitched up Wayne's sweater on the right side so it wouldn't

> "When I'm on the ice, the goalie is just a blur. It's that way for any 50-goal scorer. But if you ask a 5-goal scorer, he'll tell you the goalie is a huge blob of pads. He sees the pads, I see the net."
>
> **WAYNE GRETZKY, 1988**

get in the way when he took a shot. It helped, so Gretzky still wears his sweater that way today.

Gretzky's contributions to hockey aren't limited to assists and goals. Since his trade to the Kings, the popularity of hockey has spread across North America. The NHL has added five new teams, and five new professional hockey leagues have started up thanks to the Great One.

Although he has been slowed by injuries, Gretzky remains one of the game's finest players. In February 1996 he was traded to St. Louis where he continues to move towards the 3000-point mark, and to be the best representative hockey could have.

LEGENDS

Stan Mikita

Centre — Chicago

Stan Mikita was a legend because of his scoring ability. He could outskate most opponents to reach the puck, feather a pass to a teammate or blast a slapshot past a goaltender. At one time the high number of penalties Mikita took was also legendary. However, he soon realized he couldn't help his team from the penalty box. Mikita cleaned up his act so well that in 1967 and 1968 he won the Lady Byng Trophy for combining excellence with ''gentlemanly conduct.''

''Stosh'' is also a legend because of the hockey school he started for hearing-impaired children. When Mikita came from Czechoslovakia to Canada as a child, he couldn't speak English, so he couldn't talk with other kids. It made him realize what hearing-impaired kids go through, and he has worked to find ways to help them.

> "Hockey's given me a good life and a chance to do some good. If I didn't take advantage of that opportunity, it would be a waste. That's why I started my hockey school for hearing-impaired boys."
> **STAN MIKITA, 1977**

Guy Lafleur

Right Wing — Montreal, NY Rangers, Quebec

Guy Lafleur was a legend even before he played in the NHL. He was a superstar in the Quebec Junior League, where he was known for his speed, his shot and his ability to score important goals.

The NHL career of the "Flower" bloomed in 1974–75 when he scored 53 goals, his first of six straight 50-goal seasons. Lafleur went on to win the Hart Trophy as MVP twice and led the league in scoring three times.

In 1988, just after he was elected to the Hockey Hall of Fame, Lafleur surprised everyone by returning to play three more seasons. On his last night as an NHLer in April 1991, he summed up his career best when he said, "I didn't score for myself, I scored for the fans."

"There was no one like Lafleur when he was at his best. I saw all he did for hockey in Montreal, the goals he scored and the excitement he gave to the fans and the players he played with."

JACQUES LEMAIRE, 1984
Teammate

TEAM PLAYERS

Michel Goulet

Left Wing — Quebec, Chicago

Michel Goulet was a team player for the Nordiques not only because of his on-ice skills but also because he was a Quebec native and a natural crowd favourite. Goulet notched four 100-point seasons and four seasons with at least 50 goals. He was also a skilled playmaker, compiling more than 500 goals and 600 assists during his career.

> "As a midget hockey player, I used to go to the arena by myself at five or six o'clock in the morning to skate and work on things. Just me."
> **MICHEL GOULET, 1987**

Goulet was traded to Chicago in March 1990.

Yzerman was the youngest captain in Red Wing history when he was appointed in 1986. He was 21 at the time.

Steve Yzerman

Centre — Detroit

Steve Yzerman has been a team player in Detroit for the past 13 seasons, recording at least 100 points six times. The Red Wings missed the playoffs in 12 of the 13 seasons before he arrived, but since "Stevie Y" joined the team in 1983, Detroit has missed post-season play only twice. Yzerman is consistent and has tremendous acceleration and fast feet. He's also an intelligent player, always planning his next move on the ice.

> "Every team needs someone to step forward. As captain, I have to be the one who is always ready. I look forward to the challenge."
> **STEVE YZERMAN, 1987**

In the 1995 playoffs, Savard led Chicago in scoring with 18 points.

Denis Savard

Centre — Chicago, Montreal, Tampa Bay

During his first ten seasons in Chicago, Denis Savard was the "franchise." He represented the team in five All-Star Games and led the club in points seven times. Savard's skating skills and flashy passing made him a crowd favourite wherever he played. In 1990 he was traded to Montreal, where his dream of winning the Stanley Cup finally came true in 1993. Savard signed as a free agent with Tampa Bay in July 1993 and was traded back to Chicago in 1995.

> **"Everybody loves the way [Savard] plays hockey. But more than that, I like his attitude towards life. He's never let success go to his head. He just loves to play the game."**
>
> **ORVAL TESSIER, 1982**
> **Former Chicago Black Hawks coach**

Dale Hawerchuk

Centre — Winnipeg, Buffalo, St. Louis, Philadelphia

For nine seasons, Dale Hawerchuk was the most important member of the Winnipeg Jets. He was the Jets captain, All-Star and all-time leading scorer, notching at least 100 points in five straight seasons. But Hawerchuk is also a team player. He has recorded more assists than goals in each of his 14 NHL seasons. During the 1992–93 season, while playing for Buffalo, he recorded 80 assists, the highest total of his NHL career.

> **"As you get older you realize that it's not necessary to get two or three points a game. You learn to win instead of just putting numbers up."**
>
> **DALE HAWERCHUK, 1988**

Hawerchuk is such a consistent player that he missed only 19 games in his first 13 years.

THE ROCKET

Maurice Richard

Right Wing — Montreal

No player was as determined to succeed as Maurice "Rocket" Richard. He was injured often when he was young, and many experts predicted he'd never make it in the NHL. The Rocket spent his entire career proving those "experts" wrong.

When the Rocket was on the ice, the only thing that mattered to him was winning. And he would do whatever it took to win. He wouldn't skate around a defenceman, he'd skate through him. And when his team needed a big goal, the Rocket would get it. He had the quickest wrist shot in the league, and the strength to plough through the defence. His backhand was as hard as most players' forehand, and he could pick all four corners of the net with ease.

Richard was the first player to score 50 goals in 50 games. He scored 544 regular-season goals, which was an NHL record when he retired in 1960. And as

great as he was during the season, he was even better when the Stanley Cup was on the line. In one playoff game against Toronto, he scored an NHL record five goals. At the end of the game, he was named the first, second and third star. No one had ever seen that before. And hockey will never see a player like the Rocket again.

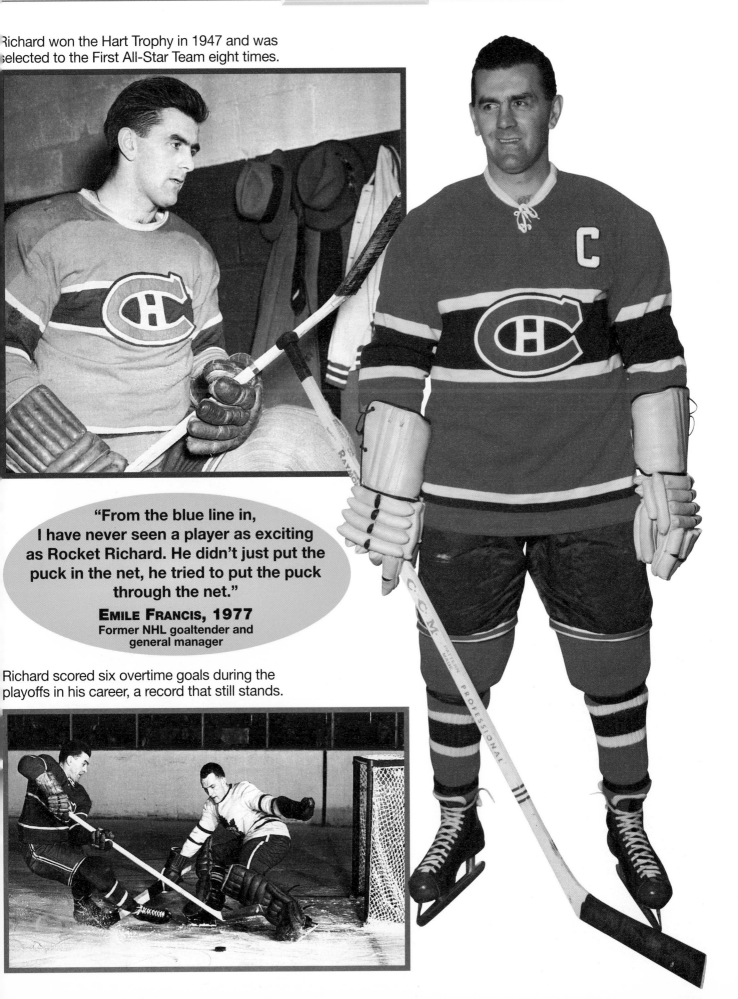

Richard won the Hart Trophy in 1947 and was selected to the First All-Star Team eight times.

"From the blue line in, I have never seen a player as exciting as Rocket Richard. He didn't just put the puck in the net, he tried to put the puck through the net."

EMILE FRANCIS, 1977
Former NHL goaltender and general manager

Richard scored six overtime goals during the playoffs in his career, a record that still stands.

CENTRES OF ATTENTION

Doug Gilmour

Centre — St. Louis, Calgary, Toronto

When he was a junior player, Doug Gilmour almost quit playing hockey because he was told he was too small to make it to the NHL. But after he read a quote that said, ''A man shows what he is by what he does with what he has,'' he decided to be the best player he could be.

As a centreman and captain, Gilmour leads by example. For him, every shift is important. He knows that winning a key face-off or breaking up a two-on-one can mean the difference between winning and losing. His hard work and determination make Gilmour a fan favourite wherever he plays.

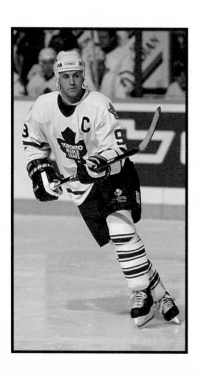

"Almost by himself, he picked the team up by the bootstraps and made it into a competitive team."

CLIFF FLETCHER, 1994
Toronto Maple Leafs general manager

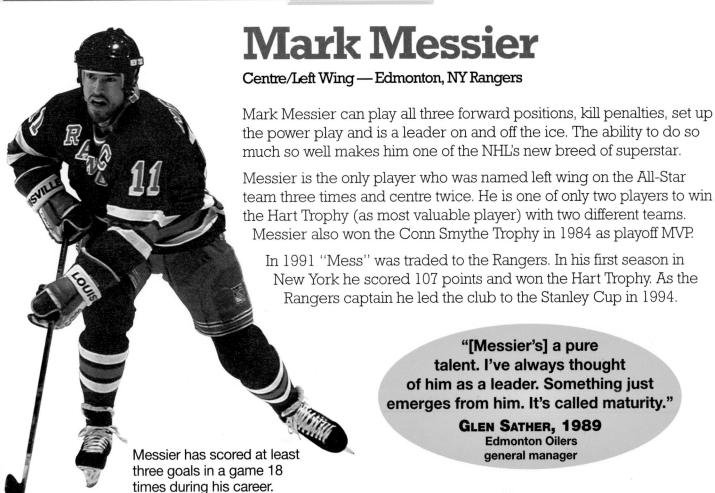

Mark Messier

Centre/Left Wing — Edmonton, NY Rangers

Mark Messier can play all three forward positions, kill penalties, set up the power play and is a leader on and off the ice. The ability to do so much so well makes him one of the NHL's new breed of superstar.

Messier is the only player who was named left wing on the All-Star team three times and centre twice. He is one of only two players to win the Hart Trophy (as most valuable player) with two different teams. Messier also won the Conn Smythe Trophy in 1984 as playoff MVP.

In 1991 ''Mess'' was traded to the Rangers. In his first season in New York he scored 107 points and won the Hart Trophy. As the Rangers captain he led the club to the Stanley Cup in 1994.

Messier has scored at least three goals in a game 18 times during his career.

> "[Messier's] a pure talent. I've always thought of him as a leader. Something just emerges from him. It's called maturity."
> **GLEN SATHER, 1989**
> Edmonton Oilers
> general manager

Bryan Trottier

Centre — NY Islanders, Pittsburgh

Bryan Trottier's dedication to his teammates and the game of hockey made him one of the best centremen in the history of the NHL. Trottier never stopped working when he was on the ice. He would kill penalties, take all the key draws and work double shifts without complaining, all of which made his teammates work harder to keep up with him. That effort helped '''Trots'' and his teammates win six Stanley Cup titles and made him the NHL's seventh all-time leading scorer.

> "I want to be remembered as the guy who gave his all on every shift. The guy who, if he missed a check, kept coming back with a second or third effort. A guy who just never quit."
> **BRYAN TROTTIER, 1985**

Trottier is now an assistant coach with the Pittsburgh Penguins.

FUTURE FABS

Peter Bondra

Right Wing — Washington

The future looks bright for Peter Bondra. After four seasons in the Czechoslovakian National League, he joined the Capitals in 1990–91. Bondra scored 37 goals in his third season. In 1994–95, this crafty skater and sneaky shooter led the league in goals.

Keith Tkachuk

Left Wing — Winnipeg

Keith Tkachuk is already one of the NHL's top forwards. And he's still getting better. Tkachuk has both the strength to mix it up in the corners and the finesse to score from the slot. This team captain was named to the NHL's Second All-Star Team in 1994–95.

John LeClair

Left Wing — Montreal, Philadelphia

With his size and speed, John LeClair is already a dominant power forward. He has the muscle to drive to the net and the talent to score when he gets there. Despite the shortened 1994–95 season, LeClair set career highs in goals and points.